Grim and Ghastly
Goings-on

by Florence Parry Heide
pictures by Victoria Chess

Lothrop, Lee & Shepard Books ━━━ *New York*

First Edition   2 3 4 5 6 7 8 9 10
Library of Congress Cataloging in Publication Data.   Heide, Florence Parry. Grim and ghastly goings-on / by Florence Parry Heide ; illustrated by Victoria Chess.   p.   cm.   Summary: A collection of twenty-one humorous poems about monsters and their ilk.   ISBN 0-688-08319-6. — ISBN 0-688-08322-6 (lib. bdg.)   1. Monsters—Juvenile poetry. 2. Children's poetry, American.   [1. Monsters—Poetry.   2. American poetry.]   I. Chess, Victoria, ill.   II. Title. PS3558.E427G7   1990   811'.54—dc20   89-8071   CIP   AC

Maybe

Maybe there's a monster
hiding in our house,
waiting in my closet
quiet as a mouse....

Maybe he is hiding
underneath my bed,
with long sharp claws and hairy arms
and a green and purple head....

Maybe he'll be looking
for someone just my size—
Maybe he's just waiting
until I close my eyes....

Maybe he eats people—
boys and girls and babies.
    If there's one thing I don't like,
    it's all those maybes!

Sir Samuel Squinn

Sir Samuel Squinn,
Sir Samuel Squinn
is very tall
and very thin.
He wears a beard
and — this is weird —
he has no skin!
It's none of our business,
Sir Samuel Squinn,
but how do you keep
your insides in?

The Snake

This is a snake: perhaps you've read of it.
The head looks like the tail of it,
the tail looks like the head of it.
And this much can be said of it —
you'd better keep ahead of it.

What You Don't Know about Food

Jelly's made from jellyfish.
Spaghetti's really worms.
Ice cream's just some dirty snow
mixed up with grimy germs.
Bread is made of glue and paste.
So are cakes and pies.
Peanut butter's filled with stuff
like squashed-up lizard eyes.
And as you eat potato chips,
remember all the while—
they're slices of the dried-up brain
of some old crocodile.

The Chair

A chair's a piece of furniture
on which you've often sat.
It has a back and arms and legs—
I'm sure you've noticed that.

A chair's a chair
and there it sits,
and sometimes you sit in it
to read, or watch TV, or sleep—
      Hey, WAIT A MINUTE!

Its arms are reaching for you.
They grab you, hold you tight.
You can't get up, you can't escape,
your eyes are wide with fright!

And now its legs are moving.
The chair is running by!
I wonder where it's taking you…?
Well…
        off you go!
           Good-bye!

Friends I'm Going to Invite to Dinner (If They Don't Eat Me First)

by Florence Parry Heide and Roxanne Heide Pierce

Burpod, Grooben, Blug, and Krodspit,
Yutchbane, Squinlisp, Dreeb, and Squog.
Snodpic, Gurglob, Swug, and Vomlit,
Bogmore, Chorkball, Froos, and Glog.

*(If he can say our names backward,
we won't eat him — until dessert!)*

Interesting Facts about Monsters

Monsters are scary!
Monsters are mean!
Monsters are hairy!
  (the ones I've seen)

Monsters will grab you
when you're alone!
Tear you to pieces!
  (the ones I've known)

Monsters say *"Awkul!"*
Monsters say *"Squird!"*
Monsters say *"Mrakkle!"*
  (the ones I've heard)

Monsters eat thumbtacks!
And don't forget,
Monsters love children!
  (the ones I've met)

The Snoffle

I'm not afraid of monsters
or any witch or bat.
I'm not afraid of skeletons
or anything like that.
I'm not afraid of tigers
or a big, man-eating shark.
I'm not afraid of giants
and I really like the dark.

> B U T

I *am* afraid of Snoffles—
They really frighten me.
A Snoffle is an awful thing,
a ghastly sight to see.
So if I see a Snoffle
I know just what I'll do.
I'll put it in a great big box
and send it off to you!

Grool

A monster named Grool
used to live down the road.
He had warts on his nose,
he had skin like a toad.
And as for his teeth,
they were long, sharp, and green —
the longest and sharpest
and greenest you've seen.

He chased all the children
each time they passed by.
He gave them bad dreams
and laughed when they'd cry.
"This cannot go on,"
they decided one day.
"Enough of this Grool!
We must chase him away!"

Now, this is the plot
that those little kids hatched:

Each got a balloon
with a long string attached.
At twelve on the dot
one dark night, they all crept
through thick, soupy fog
to the place where Grool slept.

They tied all the strings
to his feet! to his toes!
to his hair! to his ears!
to his arms! to his nose!
Grool woke with a start
and he screamed, "Don't you dare!"
But away went the rascal
Up, up, up in the air.

Now even his toenails
are gone from the scene.
And that's what you get
when you're meaner than mean!

Monster Mothers

When monster mothers get together
they brag about their babies.
The other day I heard one say,
"He got his very first fang today!"

"Mine is ugly."
"Mine is mean."
"Mine is turning
    nice and green."

"Mine's as scaly
    as a fish."
"Mine is sort of
    yellowish."

"Mine breathes fire
    and smoke and such."
"Mine has skin
    you'd hate to touch."

"Mine smells like
an old sardine."
"Mine's the weirdest
thing you've seen."

"Mine has strong and
ugly jaws."
"Mine has sharp and
dreadful claws."

"Mine has two heads."
"Mine has four!"
"Mine is learning
how to roar."

When monster mothers get together
they brag about their babies.
The other day I heard one say,
"He ate his very first kid today!"

Before You Fix Your Next Peanut Butter Sandwich — Read This:

Globb's a tiny creature who
climbs into jars and waits for you.
Yes, that is where he's often hid.
He waits till you unscrew the lid,
then he leaps out — surprise, surprise! —
and grows to an enormous size.
Then do watch out, for in a minute
he'll grab the jar and stuff you in it
and there you'll sit, alas, alack,
until *he* wants a little snack.

Hungry Jake

Jake had such an appetite!
He ate most everything in sight—
ham and steak
and chocolate cake
and pies that his Aunt Kate would bake.
And then one day by some mistake
he ate himself—
and got an awful stomachache!

A Friendly Warning

When you hear these words—
FEE FI FO FUM—
Run!
Or soon you will become
a crumb
in someone else's hungry tum.
    YUM!

Mr. Glump

Bump, bump, bumpity bump.
Up and down the basement stairs,
up and down and up again.
It must be Mr. Glump again
up and down and back again
with baskets of bones
and batches of bones,
buckets of bones
and bunches of bones.
Up the stairs and down again
it's Mr. Glump and the bones again.
Bumpity bumpity bump.

Beware of Rubber Bands

Rubber bands seem very nice
and very useful, too.
I keep some in my pocket,
and so, I'm sure, do you.
See how they stretch?
See how they squirm?
That's because each rubber band
used to be a worm.
And sometimes, very late at night,
they start to crawl around.
They creep and ooze and slither,
but they never make a sound.
They ooze along the bedroom floor.
They're stickier than glue.
They crawl up on your blanket
and swarm all over you.
Then they suck your blood out.
(I told you to Beware!)
Now all that's left of you is
skin
and bones
and hair.

The Monster in My Closet

The monster in my closet
hides there just for fun.
He shrieks and moans and rattles bones
just like a skeleton.
He always tries to scare me
(he does it as a joke).
But tonight I shouted BOO! at him
and he went up in smoke!

The Silent Type

Michael met a monster
walking down the street,
the big and strong and silent type,
the kind you sometimes meet.
Not a hi, no howdy do,
not a how's it go with you,
not a word about the weather,
not a hey, let's get together.
Not a how's your family been.
Not a smile, not a grin,
not a handshake, not a nod—
Michael thought it rather odd.
He thought the monster might be shy,
too shy to even say good-bye.
But when he landed in its tummy,
he heard the monster say: "How yummy!"

Spinach

One thing I really, really hate
is seeing spinach on my plate!
  It's oozy, it's wiggly,
  it's icky, it's squiggly,
  it's greasy, it's grimy,
  it's sticky, it's slimy,
and as it slithers ever closer
it gets slimier and grosser.

This is the thing that worries me:
I don't like spinach,
but spinach likes ME!
And as it sits upon the plate
it's thinking *I* am looking great.
Here I sit and now I see
if I don't eat it,
it will eat ME!

The Worst Thing and the Best Thing

The worst thing that can happen
is a monster in your bed.
Especially one with squishy hair
and a hole right through his head.

There isn't room for both of you,
so one of you must go.
If I were you, I'd leave him there—
Don't even say hello.

The best thing you can do
if a monster's in your bed
is just to sit up all night long
and watch TV instead.

Absolutely Nothing

Dinosaurs…
They're very, very dead, you know.
They died a zillion years ago….
But whether they're alive or dead,
there's one that hides beneath my bed.
His teeth are huge. He has big scales.
His toenails are as sharp as nails.
I hear him breathe. I hear him snore.
I hear him gnash his teeth and roar.

   My mother says, "Look here, my dear,
   there's *absolutely nothing* here!"

He's getting very hungry now….
He'll have to get a meal somehow.

   My father says, "There's nothing there.
   There's *absolutely nothing* there!"

But in the morning they will see
absolutely nothing
                    left of me!

The Sign

Monsters are an awful pain!
I've never liked them much.
But they kept getting in our house —
they liked to keep in touch.
It really wasn't all that bad,
but they got to be a bore.
The ugly sounds they made were gross —
I hated every roar.

I made a sign: YOU GUYS BEWARE —
MONSTER TRAP INSIDE.
(There isn't such a thing, of course;
about the trap, I lied.)
I put the sign outside our door.
I know it made them wince.
I scared those monsters off, I know —
I haven't seen one since!

J
811
Hei

Heide, Florence
Parry

Grim and ghastly
goings-on